Copyright © 2001 by Nord-Süd Verlag AG, Gossau Zürich, Switzerland
First published in Switzerland under the title *Ein Ei für den Osterhasen*
English translation copyright © 2001 by North-South Books Inc.

First published in the United States, Great Britain, Canada,
Australia, and New Zealand in 2001 by North-South Books,
an imprint of Nord-Süd Verlag AG, Gossau Zürich, Switzerland
Distributed in the United States by North-South Books Inc., New York

Library of Congress Cataloging-in-Publication Data is available.
The CIP catalogue record for this book is available from The British Library.

ISBN 0-7358-1442-2 (Trade Binding)
1 3 5 7 9 TB 10 8 6 4 2
ISBN 0-7358-1443-0 (Library Binding)
1 3 5 7 9 LB 10 8 6 4 2
Printed in Belgium

For more information about our books, and the authors and artists
who create them, visit our web site: www.northsouth.com

Udo Weigelt
The Easter Bunny's Baby

ILLUSTRATED BY Rolf Siegenthaler

Translated by J. Alison James

North-South Books

NEW YORK · LONDON

"Well, would you look at that," said the Easter Bunny. Someone had left him a gigantic egg. How nice, he thought. It doesn't matter that Easter isn't until tomorrow. For once, someone has brought an egg to *me*!

"Hello," called Cuckoo, who was watching from a tree.
"What a big egg you have there!"

"Yes, isn't it wonderful?" said the Easter Bunny. "I'm
going to paint it. It will be the most beautiful egg ever.
I just wonder who brought it to me."

"Well," said Cuckoo, "whoever did must be great
friends of yours."

Suddenly they heard a noise coming from the egg.

"What is that noise?" asked the Easter Bunny. "Something's moving in the egg. Why, I think this egg is alive! It needs to be hatched."

"Hatched?" asked Cuckoo, surprised.

"Of course," said the Easter Bunny. "It has to be kept warm. How lucky that you're here. You're a bird, so you can sit on the egg."

"Not me!" cried Cuckoo. "Cuckoos never sit on eggs! If I did, everyone would laugh at me."

"Ridiculous," said the Easter Bunny. "You're a bird. You can sit on the egg!"

So Cuckoo sat on the egg, but he was not happy about it.

Just then Magpie flew by. "I can't believe it!" she shrieked. "You're sitting on an egg! I thought cuckoos never did that!"

"Don't you dare tell anyone," Cuckoo said. "I'm only doing this to help the Easter Bunny."

The Easter Bunny looked at Magpie. "You can give Cuckoo a break and take turns," he said. But just then they heard a *crunch*, and a jagged crack appeared in the egg. Then another *crunch*, *crack*, and then *crumble*, *splat*, and suddenly the egg tossed Cuckoo into the air.

The egg burst open and a baby bird popped out.

"*Yup?*" asked the baby, looking at the Easter Bunny. "*Yupa!*" the baby cried, delighted. She wriggled out of the egg and ran straight to the Easter Bunny.

"I think she thinks you're her mother," said Magpie.

"Who gave me this egg anyway?" asked the Easter Bunny. "I'm not a mother bird. I don't have time for chicks. I have too much to do to get ready for Easter!"

"We didn't mean any harm," said Magpie before Cuckoo could say "*Shh!*"

"Aha!" cried the Easter Bunny. "It was you two! But why? And where did you get the egg?"

"It came from the zoo," said Magpie, embarrassed. "The ostrich had so many that we thought we could sneak one away—so that you could have an Easter egg for yourself."

"But you can't just take an egg from its nest!" cried the Easter Bunny. "Not even when it's supposed to be a present."

"Well then, we'll have to take the chick back," said Magpie with a sigh.

But no matter how hard Cuckoo and Magpie pulled, the baby ostrich just wouldn't move. She wanted to stay with the Easter Bunny.

"*Yupoo!*" cried the baby ostrich sadly. "*Yupoo!*"

"I suppose I'll have to go with you to the zoo," said the Easter Bunny finally. "But we must make sure that nobody sees me. People aren't allowed to see the Easter Bunny."

They made it to the zoo without being seen. Whenever people were near, Magpie warned the Easter Bunny, who quickly hid with the baby ostrich. Sometimes he had to hold the baby's beak, because she kept trying to call out a loud "*Yup!*"

There was a loose plank in the fence around the
ostrich pen. Magpie and Cuckoo had pushed it aside
to roll the egg out. Now they tried to push the baby
ostrich back through the opening.

But she didn't want to go. They pushed and pushed,
but the baby ostrich wouldn't budge. She was determined
to stay with her mother, the Easter Bunny.

Exhausted, the Easter Bunny gave up. "She just doesn't want to," he said in despair. "We'll have to think of something else."

"I guess we'll have to confess to her parents, Magpie," said Cuckoo nervously.

Reluctantly Magpie agreed.

They flapped over the fence and told the ostrich parents everything.

"So it was you!" cried the angry ostrich father. "Give our baby back immediately. We've been so worried!"

"That's why we're here," said Magpie. "Your baby doesn't want to come back. She thinks the Easter Bunny is her mother."

"What? What kind of nonsense is that?" said the ostrich mother. She was furious.

The ostriches rushed over to the fence. When the baby ostrich saw her parents, she hopped right into the pen. "*Yupii!*" she cried happily.

"I don't want to complain," said the Easter Bunny when they got back to his house, "but I've got a lot of eggs to paint and not much time left before Easter."

"We can help," Cuckoo said.

"That's what friends are for," said Magpie.

The Easter Bunny grinned. "Okay," he said. "But just don't give any away. That's *my* job!"